Julia
the Sleeping Beauty Fairy

To Tabitha, Verity and Thalia, from the fairies

Special thanks to
Rachel Elliot

ORCHARD BOOKS

First published in Great Britain in 2015 by Orchard Books
This edition published in 2016 by The Watts Publishing Group

3 5 7 9 10 8 6 4 2

© 2016 Rainbow Magic Limited.
© 2016 HIT Entertainment Limited.
Illustrations © Orchard Books 2015

HIT entertainment

A CIP catalogue record for this book is available from the British Library.

ISBN 978 1 40834 883 3

Printed in Great Britain

MIX
Paper from
responsible sources
FSC® C104740

FSC
www.fsc.org

The paper and board used in this book are made from wood from responsible sources

Orchard Books
An imprint of Hachette Children's Group
Part of The Watts Publishing Group Limited
Carmelite House, 50 Victoria Embankment, London EC4Y 0DZ

An Hachette UK Company
www.hachette.co.uk
www.hachettechildrens.co.uk

Julia
the Sleeping Beauty
Fairy

by Daisy Meadows

Join the Rainbow Magic Reading Challenge!

Read the story and collect your fairy points to climb the Reading Rainbow online. Turn to the back of the book for details!

This book is worth 5 points.

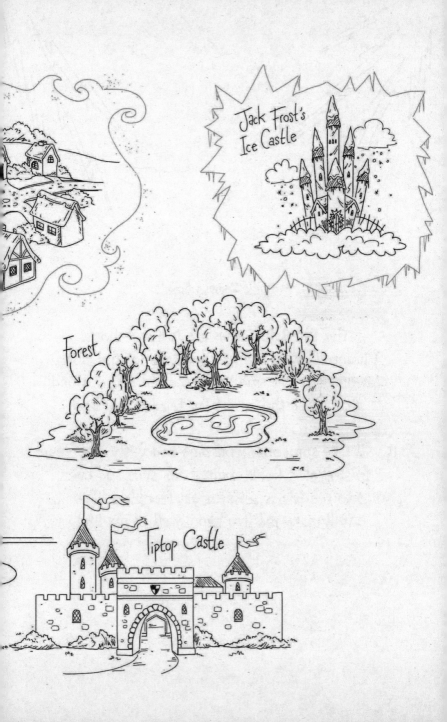

Jack Frost's
Ice Castle

Forest

Tiptop Castle

Jack Frost's Spell

The Fairytale Fairies are in for a shock!
Cinderella won't run at the strike of the clock.
No one can stop me – I've plotted and planned,
And I'll be the fairest Ice Lord in the land.

It will take someone handsome and witty and clever
To stop storybook endings for ever and ever.
But to see fairies suffer great trouble and strife,
Will make me live happily all of my life!

Contents

Over the Drawbridge

Rachel Walker rested her hand on the drawbridge chain of Tiptop Castle and looked down at the moat below. Her best friend, Kirsty Tate, was standing beside her, gazing at the elegant lawns and flower gardens that surrounded the castle. They had paused halfway across the drawbridge to admire the view.

"I feel like a princess standing here," said Kirsty in a dreamy voice. "It's just like something out of a fairy tale!"

"We're so lucky to be able to stay here for the Fairytale Festival," said Rachel, as the spring breeze ruffled her blonde hair.

It was half term, and Kirsty was staying with Rachel to share a very special treat. Tiptop Castle was a beautiful old castle on the edge of Tippington, and this year it was hosting the famous Fairytale Festival.

"I can't wait to see all the people dressed up as fairies and fairytale characters," said Kirsty.

"I wonder if we'll meet any *real* fairies," said Rachel.

The girls shared a happy smile. They

had been friends of the fairies ever since they met on Rainspell Island, and had shared many amazing adventures.

"Come on," said Kirsty. "Let's go inside."

The castle gatehouse was decorated with glimmering fairy lights. Inside was a festival organiser dressed as Puss-in-Boots. He waved his paw at Kirsty and Rachel, and then stroked his whiskers.

"Welcome to Tiptop Castle!" he said in a deep voice. "What are your names?"

The girls told him, and he ticked them off on his list. Then he gave them a big smile.

"Please enter the castle and explore with the other children until lunchtime," he said. "You can go anywhere you like and look at everything. Have fun!"

"This is going to be amazing!" said Rachel, hurrying inside and gazing around the grand entrance hall.

A chandelier hung from the ceiling,

thickly crusted with glittering crystals.
Twinkling fairy lights were twined
around the banisters of a gigantic
staircase, and suits of armour stood on
each side.

"Where shall we look first?" asked
Kirsty.

"Let's go upstairs," said Rachel, seizing
her best friend's hand. "I want to see
what a princess's bedroom looks like!"

Giggling, the girls ran up the staircase and discovered a long, wide corridor. All the doors were open, and they peeped inside each of them, gasping at what they saw. Every room was decorated in a different way. Rachel's favourite had golden furniture and red velvet curtains, while the one Kirsty liked best had a silver four-poster bed in the centre. It was surrounded by gauzy drapes and topped with a thick canopy of ivory satin. The curtains at the tall windows were azure blue.

"It looks like a mermaid's bedroom," she said with a happy sigh. "Look – the mirror is decorated with tiny silver seashells!"

All of the bedrooms took their breath away, and when they reached the end of the corridor they could hardly wait to see the rest of the castle. A second staircase led them back down to the ground floor, where they skidded across a polished oak floor into the drawing room.

"Look at the piano!" exclaimed Rachel.

A beautiful white grand piano stood beside the open French windows, and the huge mirror over the fireplace made the large room seem even bigger. Two

enormous sofas with clawed feet stood beside the fireplace. There were tall white lilies on every table.

"I wonder what's through there," said Kirsty.

She pointed to a set of double doors
that led into another room. When they
walked through, the girls discovered a
long dining room, which had a huge
wooden banqueting table in the centre.
Candelabras were spaced out along the
length of the table, and portraits of kings
and queens filled the walls.

"This is just what I imagined a
fairytale castle would be like," said
Rachel. "They must have amazing feasts
in this room!"

Just then, they heard the sound of
laughter outside the room.

"That must be some of the other
children who are here for the festival,"
said Kirsty. "Let's go and say hello."

She went to the door of the dining
room and stepped back out into the

hallway, but no one was there. Rachel joined her, and they heard footsteps running up the staircase.

"They must have gone to explore the bedrooms," said Rachel. "Never mind – I'm sure we'll meet them later. Let's see where this door leads."

She turned the handle of the next door along, and they walked into a cosy reading room. Large, squashy armchairs were positioned around the room beside polished side tables filled with snacks and jugs of water. The walls were lined with shelves of books that reached all the way to the high ceiling, and the girls gazed up at them in delight.

"Look, there are ladders so you can reach the highest shelves," said Kirsty.

"Those reading chairs look really

comfy," said Rachel. "Let's choose some books and snuggle up in them."

She turned to the nearest shelf and gave a cry of surprise. One of the books was glowing! Feeling excited, Rachel pulled the book off the shelf and out fluttered Hannah the Happy Ever After Fairy!

Fairytale Lane

"Hello, Hannah!" exclaimed Rachel and Kirsty together.

"It's wonderful to see you both!" said Hannah, her eyes shining with pleasure. "I've come because I know how much you like reading, so I have a surprise for you."

She waved her wand, and there was a
tinkling sound as silver fairy dust sparkled
around them. The
girls shrank
to fairy size
and felt their
gossamer
wings
fluttering on
their backs. They
were filled with a delicious sense of
excitement as they realised that Hannah
was taking them to Fairyland.

In the blink of an eye, the reading
room had disappeared. Rachel and
Kirsty were standing on a narrow,
cobbled lane. There were four pretty
cottages spaced out along the lane, with
thatched roofs and roses and honeysuckle

twining around the doors. The smoke
that came from the chimneys sparkled
in all the colours of the rainbow, and a
mouth-watering smell of freshly baked
cakes hung in the air.

"Welcome to Fairytale Lane," said
Hannah.

As she spoke, the cottage doors opened
and four beautiful fairies peered out.

When they saw the girls, they came
hurrying over to say hello.

"These are the Fairytale Fairies,"
said Hannah with a beaming smile.
"Meet Julia the Sleeping Beauty Fairy,
Eleanor the Snow White Fairy, Faith
the Cinderella Fairy and Lacey the Little
Mermaid Fairy."

"It's lovely to meet you all," said

Rachel, smiling at the fairies. "I didn't know that there were Fairytale Fairies!"

"Oh yes," said Julia, whose auburn hair was tied in a loose bun. "Each of us takes care of a fairy tale and the characters in it."

"Without our care, the characters could get lost and the stories would be empty," added Eleanor.

Faith squeezed Kirsty's hand and smiled shyly.

"Hannah told us how much you like fairy tales," she said. "We have a present for you."

Lacey pulled a book from behind her back and handed it to the girls. It was so sparkly that it was hard to know whether it was gold or silver, and the title was written in swirly pink lettering:

The Fairies' Book of Fairy Tales

A silky pink
ribbon bookmark
dangled from the
spine.

"Oh, thank you!"
said Kirsty in a
thrilled voice. "It's
the most beautiful
book I've ever seen!"

Eagerly, Rachel opened the book
and turned to the first story. But to her
astonishment, the page was completely
blank. She turned some more pages, and
found that they were all blank.

"I don't understand," said Julia, gazing
at the book in dismay.

She glanced over at her cottage
window, and then let out a cry of alarm.

"My magical jewellery box!" she exclaimed. "I always keep it on the sitting-room windowsill, but it's not there!"

Exchanging worried looks, the other three fairies dashed into their cottages. Seconds later they came back out, looking pale and anxious. All their magical objects had gone missing!

"This explains why *The Fairies' Book of Fairy Tales* is blank," said Julia with a groan. "But where could our magical objects be?"

"I can guess," said Kirsty suddenly.

She pointed to the end of the lane, where four goblins were sneaking away! Each one of them had something clutched in his hands.

"They've stolen the magical objects!" Rachel guessed aloud. "Come on, we can catch them if we're quick!"

The girls zoomed off through the air as fast as their wings could flutter, but before they could reach the goblins, Jack Frost leaped out in front of them!

"Halt!" he snarled. "Those fairy objects are mine now, and I'm taking them to the human world!"

"No," said Kirsty, trying to sound brave. "They belong to the Fairytale Fairies. You should give them back."

"Tough luck," Jack Frost snapped. "I've had enough of silly fairies and princesses. From now on, all fairy tales are going to be about me, me, ME!"

The goblins had stopped at the end of the lane, and they gave a big cheer when they heard what he said.

"Please stop!" cried Julia, flying up to join the girls. "Just think of all the children who won't have fairy tales to read."

"I don't care," said Jack Frost with a sneer. "And what's more, I'm going to start with *Sleeping Beauty*. From now on, it's going to be called *Sleeping Jack Frost!*"

As the girls gave horrified gasps, there was a thunderclap and, with a bolt of icy magic, Jack Frost and the goblins disappeared to the human world.

A Wooden Bed

Hannah and the Fairytale Fairies flew up to join Julia and the girls.

"Jack Frost has taken your magical objects to the human world," said Kirsty. "He's planning to make your fairy tales all about him, starting with *Sleeping Beauty*."

The fairies looked very upset.

"That means that the fairy tale characters must be in the human world too," said Julia. "We have to get our magical objects back and return the characters to their stories, or fairy tales will be ruined forever."

"Please let us help you," said Rachel. "We can't let Jack Frost do this to our favourite stories!"

The Fairytale Fairies looked very grateful, and Hannah nodded.

"I think it would be a good idea to help Julia first," she said.

"Oh yes, please," said Julia. "I need my magic jewellery box to rescue Sleeping Beauty and return her to her story."

"Then we should go back to the human world straight away and start searching," said Kirsty.

Julia nodded and, with a wave of her
wand, she whisked all three of them
back to Tiptop Castle. The girls found
themselves standing in the cosy reading
room, human-sized again. Julia fluttered
between them.

"Where shall we start looking?" she
asked in a breathless voice.

Before the girls could reply, they heard laughter and giggles coming from the big dining room next door.

"I wonder what's so funny," said Kirsty.

"Let's go and find out," Rachel suggested. "Julia, you can hide in my pocket if you like."

Julia slipped into Rachel's pocket, and then the girls ran through to the dining room. They found a crowd of giggling children wearing fairytale costumes – from frog princes to enchanted princesses and fairy godmothers. They were all standing around the long banqueting table, and Rachel and Kirsty had to stand on tiptoes to see what they were laughing at.

A beautiful young woman was lying in

the centre of the banqueting table, fast asleep. She was wearing a long golden gown with huge puffed sleeves, and her raven-black hair spread around her head in long, silky coils. Her skin looked as smooth as velvet.

"How on earth can she sleep through all this laughter?" Kirsty wondered aloud. "Who is she?"

"She's one of the festival organisers, of course," said a rather pompous girl dressed as a pumpkin. "Why else would she be wearing fancy dress?"

"It's a bit strange that she's fallen asleep on the table," said Rachel.

"Perhaps she's been working hard to prepare for the festival," Kirsty suggested.

"Come on, we have to start searching for
the magical objects."

But as they moved towards the door,
Julia peeped out of Rachel's pocket and
then let out a squeak of surprise.

"That's not a festival organiser,"
whispered the little fairy. "That's
Sleeping Beauty!"

Rachel and Kirsty stared at the
princess, hardly able to believe that they
were looking at the real Sleeping Beauty.
Then Kirsty noticed something that made
her heart thump. Four pairs of large,
green feet were poking out from under
the dining table!

"Look!" Kirsty whispered, nudging Rachel. "Do those look like goblin feet to you?"

"Definitely," said Rachel with a frown. "Come on, let's get closer."

None of the other children had noticed the feet – they were all too busy giggling at Sleeping Beauty. Rachel and Kirsty crouched down beside the table and listened.

"My arms are aching from carrying that big girl," complained a scratchy voice.

"Mine too, said a deeper voice. "I don't see why we had to carry her all the way down from the big bedroom."

"Because Jack Frost needed the four-poster bed to be Sleeping Jack Frost, of course," squawked a third goblin voice.

"Talking of Jack Frost, shouldn't we get back upstairs?" said a fourth goblin, sounding nervous. "He might want something and he'll be ever so cross if we're not there."

"They're coming out," whispered Kirsty.

There was a scrabbling sound under the table, and then the girls saw the four goblins crawling out from under the table on their stomachs. They scuttled across the floor, unnoticed by the other children, and slipped out of the dining room.

"Quickly, let's follow them," said Rachel. "They can lead us to Jack Frost and the magical objects!"

Grumbling Goblins

Kirsty and Rachel hurried out of the dining room, and bumped straight into the man dressed as Puss-in-Boots, who had met them at the entrance.

"Aha, Rachel and Kirsty," he said. "Are you having fun exploring?"

The girls groaned inwardly as the goblins disappeared up the stairs.

"It's been really exciting so far," said Rachel. "We were just going to have another look upstairs."

"That's fine," said Puss-in-Boots. "But remember, we'll be serving lunch in the garden, so don't miss it!"

He walked on, and Rachel and Kirsty ran up the stairs. The landing was empty.

"They've gone into a bedroom," said Kirsty. "But which one?

Then they heard footsteps on the stairs behind them. They turned around and

44

saw a handsome young man dressed as
a prince coming towards them. He wore
a large felt hat with a
feather in it, and
his tunic was
made of gold
brocade.

"Good
morning," he
said, pulling
off his hat and
sweeping a low
bow. "I am Prince
Humphrey."

Rachel and Kirsty smiled at him,
guessing that he was another festival
organiser.

"We already know about the lunch
outside," said Rachel.

"Lunch outside?" repeated Prince Humphrey in a puzzled voice. "I don't know what you mean. I'm looking for Sleeping Beauty."

"That's the real prince from the fairy tale!" whispered Julia from Rachel's pocket.

"Oh my goodness, you've come to wake her up with a kiss, haven't you?" asked Kirsty in excitement. "She's downstairs in the dining room."

The prince darted back down the stairs, and the girls shared a smile before they hurried across the landing towards the bedrooms.

"Wait!" said Julia suddenly. "It will be easier to hide from Jack Frost if you are fairies too. Can you find a place to hide so that I can transform you?"

There was a large statue of a fairy on the landing, and Rachel pulled Kirsty behind it. Then Julia flew out and waved her wand. Instantly, the girls were fluttering their beautiful wings and hovering beside Julia. They checked that no one was coming and then zoomed towards the bedrooms.

"The goblins mentioned a four-poster bed," said Rachel. "So Jack Frost must be in the silver-and-blue room that you liked best, Kirsty."

The three fairies flew to the open door of the bedroom and peeped in. Jack Frost was lying on the beautiful silver bed, wearing a long blue nightgown and an old-fashioned nightcap. His head was buried in a plump pillow, and Rachel noticed that his wand was lying on the ornate bedside table. The four goblins were lying on the floor around the bed, fidgeting and kicking each other. Each of them had a thin pillow, but they didn't look very sleepy.

"Get your foot out of my mouth, you clumsy oaf!" squawked one.

"Shan't!" said another, and then let out a yell of pain. "You bit me!"

Suddenly, Jack Frost
sat bolt upright as if
there were a spring
inside him.

"You lot are too
noisy!" he roared
at the four goblins.
"How am I supposed
to sleep with all this
racket? SHUT UP!"

He flopped back onto the bed as the
goblins froze with fear. Julia fluttered
into the room and beckoned to Rachel
and Kirsty, who followed her at once.
They all perched on top of the satin bed
canopy.

"My pillow's too bumpy," muttered
one of the goblins.

"Mine's too squashy," said another.

"I'll have it," said a third, snatching at the pillow.

Rachel, Kirsty and Julia lay on their tummies and peered over the canopy.

"Any sign of my magical jewellery box?" whispered Julia.

The girls shook their heads. All they could see was the tassel on Jack Frost's nightcap, and the squirming green limbs of the four goblins.

"It's no use," said Jack Frost. "I can't sleep."

"We can't sleep either," wailed the goblins.

"Then you might as well give me your pillows," said Jack Frost. "Hand them over NOW!"

"It's not fair!" wailed the goblins as Jack Frost snatched their pillows. "You've already taken our blankets."

"I don't care about fair!" Jack Frost bellowed. "I care about ME! Now, sing me a lullaby."

"Oh no," groaned Rachel, who had heard the goblins singing before. "We might need earplugs."

Jack Frost sank back into the mound of pillows and the goblins linked arms and started to sing.

"Rock-a-bye Jack Frost on the soft bed.

When he shouts loud, it fills us with dread.

*When he
gets cross, the
snowflakes will fall.
He'll keep our
blankets, pillows and all."*

Their squawky voice made the fairies
wince. Jack Frost pulled his nightcap
down over his ears and plumped up his
pillow.

"Idiots!" he snarled. "Call that a
lullaby? Just shut up and lie down."

"Look!" hissed Kirsty.

As Jack Frost plumped up his pillow,
he revealed the corner of an engraved
wooden box hidden underneath it. Julia
sharply drew in her breath.

"That's my magical jewellery box!"
she exclaimed. "Thank goodness we've
found it! But how can we get it back?"

Pillow Fight!

The goblins lay down again, grumbling under their breath. The fairies could only catch a few muttered words.

"Stupid hard floors."

"No pillows."

"It's a bit nippy."

An idea suddenly popped into Rachel's head, and she turned to Kirsty and Julia with excitement in her eyes.

"Everyone loves a pillow fight," she whispered. "We just need a few more pillows…"

Julia laughed and flicked her wand. At once, a huge mound of soft pillows appeared beside the goblins, who gave loud cheers and flung themselves into the pile. The fairies zoomed down from the

canopy and Julia returned Kirsty and Rachel to their human form. Rachel picked up a pillow and gently threw it at the nearest goblin. He turned and glared at her for a moment, then a huge, toothy smile spread across his face.

"PILLOW FIGHT!" he yelled.

Seconds later, pillows were whizzing through the air as fast as the goblins could hurl them. They were throwing them at each other as well as at the girls, and Jack Frost started jumping up and down on the bed in a rage.

"Stop it!" he shrieked. "I'm trying to sleep!"

The girls couldn't help giggling as they flung pillows back at the goblins. Julia retreated to the canopy and magicked up more and more pillows, until the floor was completely hidden under them.

Feeling brave, Rachel took aim and hurled a pillow at Jack Frost's head. His nightcap came off and he shook his fist at her.

"We have to make him join in the fight and get him away from the magical jewellery box," Rachel panted.

Kirsty grabbed another pillow and flung it at Jack Frost with all her might. He fell over backwards and then bounced up again, scarlet with fury.

"You pesky humans!" he screeched. "I'll make you sorry for disturbing me!"

He snatched up his plump pillow and threw it at them as hard as he could, revealing the magical jewellery box lying on the mattress. The girls ducked the pillow and Rachel dived towards the bed. But Jack Frost was too quick for her. With a sneering laugh he snatched up the jewellery box, jumped down from the bed and sprinted out of the room.

"After him!" Julia cried. "We mustn't let him get away again!"

Rachel and Kirsty pelted after Jack Frost, who had hitched his nightgown up over his knees so that he could run faster. Behind them, they could hear the patter of goblin feet. Julia zoomed above their heads.

"He's going downstairs!" she called. "Faster!"

The girls hurtled downstairs and chased Jack Frost into the dining room. He skidded around the enormous table and stood in the far corner, panting. The girls stopped to catch their breath too, and then noticed that Sleeping Beauty was no longer lying on the table. She was sitting up, and her lovely eyes were open. She was awake! Prince Humphrey was standing beside the table and holding her hand. They both looked at Jack Frost and the girls in surprise.

"Where are the other children?" asked Rachel, looking around.

"They went outside to have some lunch," said Prince Humphrey.

Sleeping Beauty blinked a few times and then spoke in a soft, musical voice.

"I'm a little confused," she said. "Where is my palace? Shouldn't I be in my bed?"

"It's all Jack Frost's fault," said Kirsty, looking at the Ice Lord. "He stole Julia's magical jewellery box. Without it, you can't get back into your own story! We've been trying to get it from him."

"In that case, please allow us to help you," said Sleeping Beauty.

She jumped down from the table at once, and Prince Humphrey turned to face Jack Frost.

"You'll never catch me," said Jack
Frost, curling his lip. "A couple of little
girls and two weedy fairytale characters
are no match for the great Jack Frost!"

"We'll see about that," said Sleeping
Beauty in a commanding voice. "I am
a princess, and I insist that you give me
that jewellery box right now!"

The Magical Jewellery Box

Prince Humphrey ran towards the Ice Lord, who darted around the table in the opposite direction. Sleeping Beauty blocked his way, and he dodged sideways, diving under the table and scrambling out near the door. But Rachel and Kirsty were there, and he was forced to duck back under the

table again. Sleeping Beauty, Prince
Humphrey and the girls each crouched
down at one side of the table.

"There's no way out," said Rachel,
remembering what she had noticed in the
bedroom. "Your wand is upstairs where
you left it, so you can't escape by magic.
Give us the jewellery box and we will let
you go."

Just then, they heard the heavy patter
of bare feet behind them, and the four
goblins appeared in the doorway.

"Just in the nick of time," yelled Jack
Frost. "CATCH!"

He tossed the magical jewellery box
over Kirsty's head towards the door. But
Kirsty sprang into the air, reaching her
hands high above her head.

"Noooo!" shrieked Jack Frost as

Kirsty's right hand
closed around the box.

"Yes!" Rachel
cheered in delight.
"You didn't know
that Kirsty's the best
netball player in her
school!"

Smiling with relief, Kirsty handed the
magical jewellery box to Julia, and it
immediately shrank to fairy size. Jack
Frost jumped up in fury and banged his
head on the underside of the table. A
large lump appeared under his spiky hair.

"You interfering, annoying humans!"
he snapped, clutching his head and
crawling out from under the table. "Just
you wait until I've got my wand in
my hand!"

"It's too late," said Rachel. "Julia has her magical object back."

Jack Frost stuck out his tongue at her and then stomped out of the room with the goblins.

"Thank you both for all your help," said Julia, holding her magical jewellery box close to her heart. "I'll never forget your kindness – or your courage!"

She blew them each a kiss and then disappeared back to Fairyland in a shimmering haze of fairy dust.

Prince Humphrey clasped Sleeping
Beauty in his arms as they started to
shimmer and fade.

"Goodbye!" Sleeping Beauty called.
"Thank you!"

Moments later they had gone and the
girls were alone in the
dining room.

"Do you think
they've returned
to their story?"
asked Kirsty.

"I hope so,"
said Rachel as
her stomach gave
a loud rumble. "But
right now, I think we
should go and get some lunch with the
others!"

That night, Rachel and Kirsty felt like princesses as they got ready for their first night at Tiptop Castle. Their bedroom was at the top of one of the tall castle towers, and the tiny arched windows looked out over the glassy lake and the beautiful moonlit gardens.

"This is the most incredible room I've ever slept in," said Kirsty.

She gazed around at the dark wooden furniture, which had been polished until it gleamed, and the single four-poster beds with their drapes and canopies. Rachel flopped down on her bed and yawned, snuggling back against her feathery pillow.

"It's been a wonderful day," she said. "Oh, what's this? There's something hard under my pillow... "

She reached her
hand under her
pillow and drew
out the sparkling
book that the
fairies had given
them – *The Fairies'*
Book of Fairy Tales.

Kirsty gave a gasp of delight.

"I'd forgotten about our present in all
the excitement," she said. "I wonder how
it got there?"

"Magic," said Rachel with a grin.

Kirsty joined Rachel on her bed,
and with their fingers crossed they
opened the book and turned to the
first story. They were relieved to see
the words 'Sleeping Beauty' at the
top of the page. The story was in the

book again, and Sleeping Beauty and her prince were both back where they belonged.

"Let's read it before bed," Rachel suggested.

The girls loved the story and had read it together often. But this time, when they read about the party that the King and Queen threw to celebrate Sleeping Beauty being born, they discovered something new. Kirsty leaned closer to the picture.

"Look," she said in an awed t
"Look at Sleeping Beauty's seven
godmothers."

Rachel leaned closer too, and then
shared a thrilled smile with her best
friend. The fairy godmothers were the
Princess Fairies!

When they reached 'happily ever after',
Rachel couldn't resist turning the page to
see if the next story had reappeared too.

"It's blank," she said with a sigh.
"The other stories are still missing, and
we have three more Fairytale Fairies to
help."

Kirsty put her arm around Rachel's
shoulders and smiled at her.

"Don't worry," she said. "As long as
best friends like us stick together, I know
that we can make a happy ending!"

Meet the
Fairytale Fairies

Kirsty and Rachel are going to a Fairytale Festival!
Can they help get the Fairytale Fairies' magical objects
back from Jack Frost, before he ruins all the stories?

Now it's time for Kirsty and Rachel to help...

Eleanor the Snow White Fairy

Read on for a sneak peek...

When Kirsty Tate opened her eyes, for a moment she couldn't remember where she was. She gazed up at the canopy that hung over her four-poster bed. A spring breeze had wafted open the gauzy curtains, and the sun lit up the white dressing table with its gold and silver swirls. On the dressing table lay a book with a sparkling cover – *The Fairies' Book of Fairy Tales*.

A smile spread across Kirsty's face as she remembered everything that had happened the day before. She sat up and looked across to where her best friend,

Rachel Walker, was still fast asleep.

"Rachel, wake up," she said in a gentle voice. "It's our second day at Tiptop Castle!"

Rachel opened her eyes and gave Kirsty a sleepy smile. They were staying in a beautiful old castle on the outskirts of Tippington, where the Fairytale Festival was being held. Their bedroom was at the top of a tower of the castle, and the girls had agreed that it was fit for a princess – or two!

"What are you going to wear today?" asked Kirsty, hopping out of bed and opening the enormous wardrobe where they had hung their clothes.

"How about our fairy dresses?" suggested Rachel, swinging her legs out of bed. "It'd be fun to join in with everyone else."

The day before, all the festival organisers had been wearing fairytale fancy dress. Kirsty clapped her hands together.

"That's a great idea," she said, "especially after our Fairyland visit yesterday!"

As they pulled on their beautiful fairy dresses, they talked about the adventure they had shared with Julia the Sleeping Beauty Fairy.

Read **Eleanor the Snow White Fairy** to find out what adventures are in store for Kirsty and Rachel!

Calling all parents, carers and teachers!
The Rainbow Magic fairies are here to help
your child enter the magical world of reading.
Whatever reading stage they are at, there's
a Rainbow Magic book for everyone!
Here is Lydia the Reading Fairy's guide to
supporting your child's journey at all levels.

Starting Out

1 Our Rainbow Magic Beginner Readers are perfect for first-time readers who are just beginning to develop reading skills and confidence. Approved by teachers, they contain a full range of educational levelling, as well as lively full-colour illustrations.

Developing Readers

2 Rainbow Magic Early Readers contain longer stories and wider vocabulary for building stamina and growing confidence. These are adaptations of our most popular Rainbow Magic stories, specially developed for younger readers in conjunction with an Early Years reading consultant, with full-colour illustrations.

Going Solo

3 The Rainbow Magic chapter books - a mixture of series and one-off specials - contain accessible writing to encourage your child to venture into reading independently. These highly collectible and much-loved magical stories inspire a love of reading to last a lifetime.

www.rainbowmagicbooks.co.uk

"Rainbow Magic got my daughter reading chapter books. Great sparkly covers, cute fairies and traditional stories full of magic that she found impossible to put down" - Mother of Edie (6 years)

"Florence LOVES the Rainbow Magic books. She really enjoys reading now" Mother of Florence (6 years)

The Rainbow Magic Reading Challenge

Well done, fairy friend – you have completed the book!
This book was worth 5 points.

See how far you have climbed on the **Reading Rainbow**
on the Rainbow Magic website below.

The more books you read, the more points you will get,
and the closer you will be to becoming a Fairy Princess!

How to get your Reading Rainbow
1. Cut out the coin below
2. Go to the Rainbow Magic website
3. Download and print out your poster
4. Add your coin and climb up the Reading Rainbow!

There's all this and lots more at
www.rainbowmagicbooks.co.uk

You'll find activities, competitions, stories, a special
newsletter and complete profiles of all the
Rainbow Magic fairies. Find a fairy with your name!